The Pillow Fairy

Written by Marcia G. Riley
Illustrated by Joni E. Patterson

ISBN: 1477570713
ISBN-13: 9781477570715
Library of Congress Control Number: 2012909867
CreateSpace, North Charleston, SC

For Justin and Matt, who made the Pillow Fairy such a magical time.
To Steve, for all of his love and support.
And to my dear friends and family, whose encouragement
helped make *The Pillow Fairy* a reality.

Dedicated to all the mommies and daddies who never sleep alone...

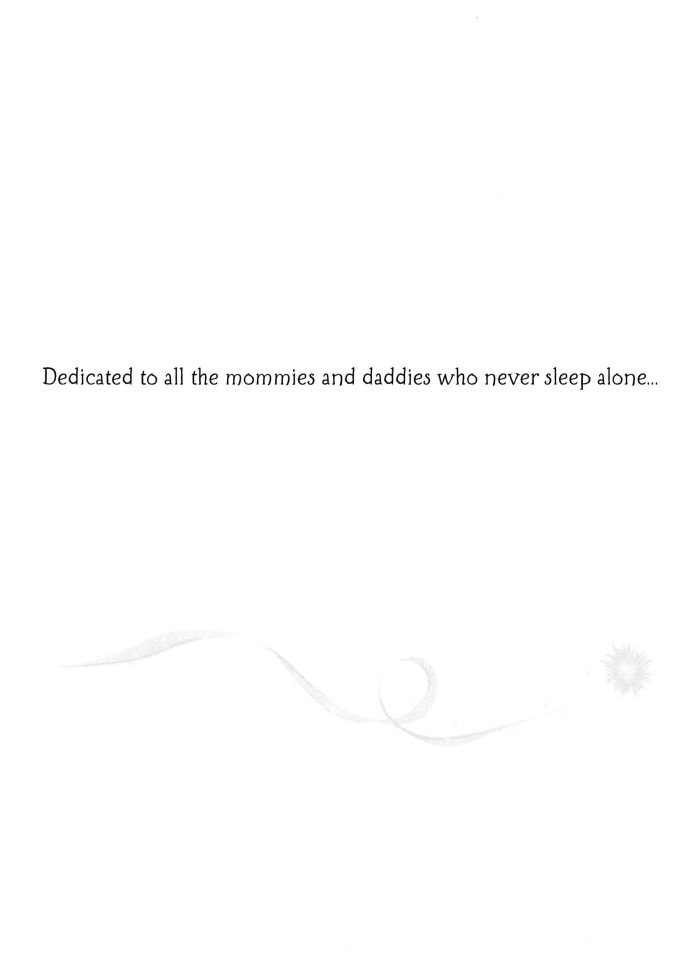

There once was a little boy named Matt.

He liked to do all the things that happy, active three year olds do...

He liked to ride his bike,

play with his dog Gypsy,

and eat macaroni and cheese.

But the one thing Matt did NOT like to do was...

Sleep in his own bed—*all by himself.*

Matt's mommy and daddy had to lie down with him every night.

Either in his bed....

or in theirs

One night as Matt was getting into bed, his mother looked outside. She saw a tiny bright light hovering outside Matt's window. Suddenly, she remembered a story that her mother had told her when she was a little girl.

"Matt, the pillow fairy is outside your window!" she exclaimed.

"The pillow fairy?" Matt asked, "What's the pillow fairy?"

"The pillow fairy," Mommy excitedly explained, "is a little fairy that visits boys and girls who sleep in their own bed—*all by themselves.* When they wake up in the morning, they look under their pillow, and they find that she's left them a little surprise."

"How do you know?" Matt asked cautiously.

"Why, the pillow fairy came to my house when I was your age."

"Did she leave you little presents?" Matt whispered, his eyes open wide with excitement.

"Yes, but only when I went to bed and woke up, in my own bed, *all by myself*," Mommy said.

"Hurry, Matt, you'd better go to sleep before she moves onto the next house," Mommy warned.

Matt quickly jumped into bed.

Mommy kissed him, shut off the light, and quietly closed the door...

The next morning, Mommy and Daddy were awakened by excited shouts from Matt's room.

"Mommy, Daddy, come see what the pillow fairy left me!"

Matt held up a shiny metallic sticker in his hand.

"Where did that come from?" Daddy asked.

"From the pillow fairy," Matt announced proudly. "She leaves little presents under your pillow, if you sleep in your own bed— *all by yourself.*"

Every night from then on, Matt and Mommy would get ready for bed.

Mommy would tuck him in and answer Matt's questions about the pillow fairy.

"What does she look like?"

"How big is she?"

"Can I see her?"

Mommy would look out the window, and when she saw the tiny bright light at the end of their driveway, she would pull down the shade, give Matt a kiss, and close the bedroom door...

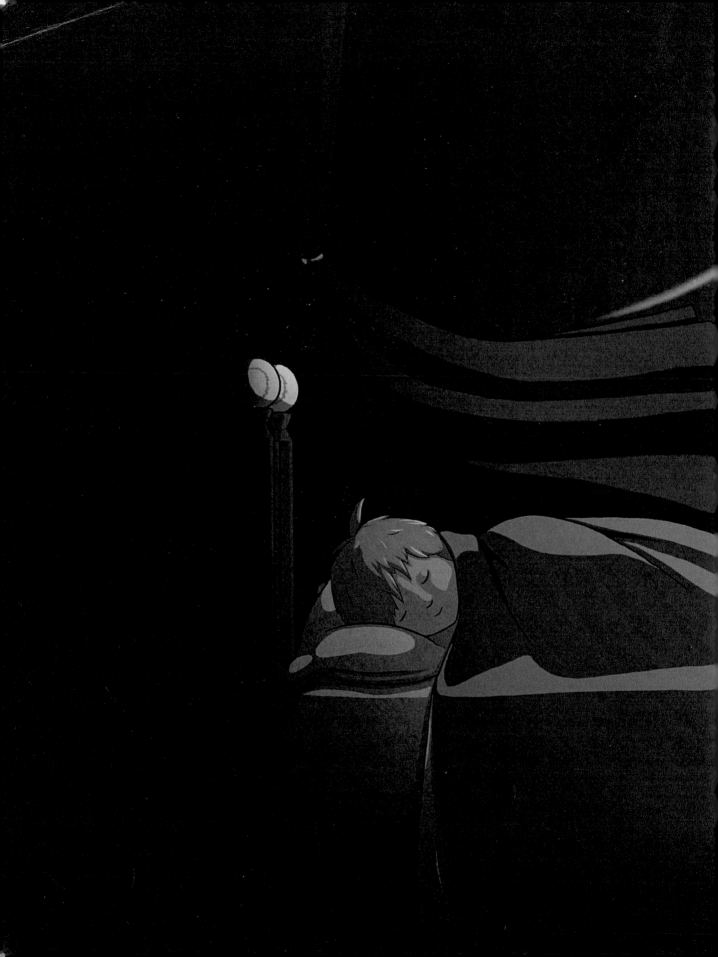

And every morning, Matt would pick up his pillow to see what magical gift the pillow fairy had left him:

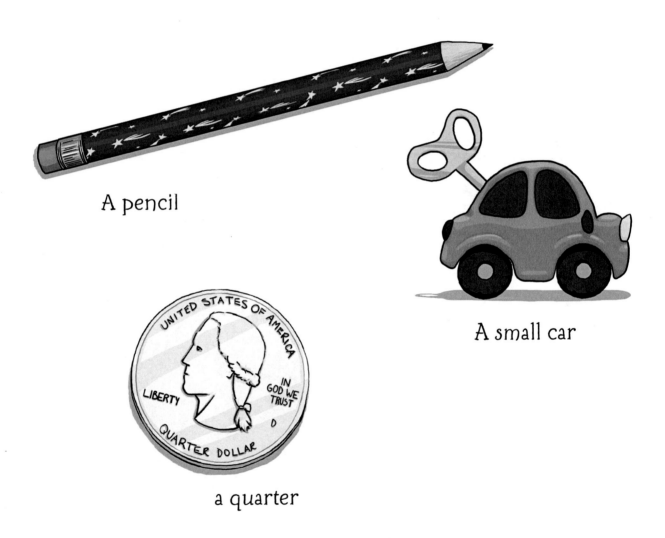

A pencil

A small car

a quarter

Sometimes she would also leave a little note.

Dear Matt,
 Sorry, but I'm all
OUT OF BRONTOSAURUSES.
I hope this Stegosaurus
is O.K.. You did A
Great Job of going
to Bed Tonight.
 Love,
 PILLOW
 FAIRY

Several months passed, and Matt had been
sleeping in his own bed-all by himself.

One morning, Matt woke up to find that nothing had been left under his pillow.

"Mommy, Daddy, the pillow fairy didn't come!"
Matt wailed loudly.

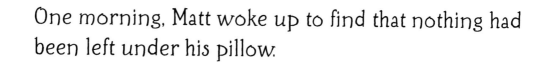

"I knew this would happen," Mommy replied.

"Why didn't she come?" Matt asked tearfully.

You have been sleeping in your own bed-*all by yourself*,"
Mommy explained gently. "You don't need the pillow fairy
anymore. She has moved on to help other little boys and girls."

Matt looked outside the window and thought about
that for a moment. "Will she ever come and see
me again?" he asked hopefully.

"Oh yes, she will stop by from time-to-time to check on you. You never know when she will come by to be sure that you are still sleeping in your own bed-*all by yourself.* You'll know she was here because she will leave you something underneath your pillow."

Matt was silent for a moment, absorbing all that Mommy was saying.

Suddenly a big smile dashed across his face.

"When she does, I'll be ready!" Matt laughed.

And with that, he went off to play.

Made in the USA
San Bernardino, CA
18 February 2016